GW01019264

Happy Birthday Johnny –
but don't quote me on That!
Love
Michel 2001

gay sex quotes

gay sex quotes

Celebrities talk about men who love men

Edited by John Erich & Gerry Kroll

alyson
books

LOS ANGELES • NEW YORK

MANUFACTURED IN THE UNITED STATES OF AMERICA.
PRINTED ON ACID-FREE PAPER.

THIS TRADE PAPERBACK ORIGINAL IS PUBLISHED BY ALYSON PUBLICATIONS INC.,
P.O. BOX 4371, LOS ANGELES, CALIFORNIA 90078-4371.
DISTRIBUTION IN THE UNITED KINGDOM BY TURNAROUND PUBLISHER SERVICES LTD.
UNIT 3 OLYMPIA TRADING ESTATE, COBURG ROAD, WOOD GREEN,
LONDON N22 6TZ ENGLAND.

FIRST EDITION: MAY 1998

02 01 00 99 98   10 9 8 7 6 5 4 3 2 1

ISBN 1-55583-463-9

LIBRARY OF CONGRESS CATALOGING-IN-PUBLICATION DATA
    GAY SEX QUOTES : CELEBRITIES TALK ABOUT MEN WHO LOVE MEN / EDITED BY
JOHN ERICH & GERRY KROLL. — 1ST ED.
        ISBN 1-55583-463-9
        1. GAYS—QUOTATIONS. 2. HOMOSEXUALITY—QUOTATIONS, MAXIMS, ETC.
    3. QUOTATIONS, ENGLISH. I. ERICH, JOHN. II. KROLL, GERRY.
    PN6084.G35G39 1998
    305.38'96642—DC21   98-13722 CIP

PHOTO CREDITS
PAGE VIII: MUNYAN/STUDIO 1435; PAGES 16, 108: J.P. STUDIOS; PAGES 28, 90, 140:
JOHNATHAN BLACK; PAGE 42: MATT BAUER

Contents

Let's Talk About Sex

Even on the most mundane of topics, people say the darndest things. But when it comes to the topic of sex between men—in its many controversial forms, shapes, and variations—folks can *really* raise some eyebrows with their comments.

In this compendium of insights, witticisms, and accidentally profound offhand comments, a fascinating cross section of celebrities expounds on man-to-man intimacies. From the big-screen stars of Hollywood to the policy makers of Washington, D.C., and the sex professionals of adult video, the people included here will amaze and amuse you with their thoughts on other people's private acts. Lucky us—some folks are never at a loss for words.

1 Men Versus Women

"Most of my male friends are gay, and that seems perfectly natural to me. I mean, who wouldn't like cock?"

—**Valerie Perrine,** *quoted in Leigh Rutledge's* The New Gay Book of Lists

"We're all homosexual—fortunately! It's part of life, and if you don't take advantage of it, you lose out on a lot of things."

—**Gérard Depardieu**

"I often say how great it would be to be gay because it would be so much easier to get a guy. Guys are much less into a head trip.... Before AIDS you could walk into a bar, and there was a glory hole. You could put your penis through a piece of wood, and somebody would suck it."

—**Howard Stern**

3

"Millions of people do it, and it's been around since the beginning of time, so nothing's really wrong with being gay or bisexual. There's things about a woman I enjoy and things about a man I enjoy."

—*Porn star* **Bo Summers**

"Somehow or other, having that feminine persona makes it much easier for straight guys to deal with having sex with you if you're a man."

—**Boy George**

"The real clue to your sex orientation lies in your romantic feelings rather than in your sexual feelings. If you are really gay, you are able to fall in love with a man, not just enjoy having sex with him."

—**Christopher Isherwood,** *quoted in Leigh Rutledge's* The New Gay Book of Lists

"There were times when I thought I was a girl stuck in a boy's body. But after puberty I was quite happy to be a boy. Although when I was 10 I did tongue-kiss Tiny, the girl across the street. I also took her panties off—mainly because I wanted them for myself!"

—**RuPaul** *in* GQ

"There are famous sheep out in Utah or somewhere where about 10% of the males prefer to have sex with other males. And this is a lifelong thing, not just a one-shot thing. People who say that homosexuality isn't natural are just wrong."

—**Simon LeVay**

"If you want your lover to treat you as a woman while you're in bed, fine, go ahead and do it. If you want him to string you up or chain you down or if you want to have sex while eating bananas, whatever, do it. There's a kind of divine irresponsibility in the bedroom, and that sense of following your fantasies—of generating them, nourishing them, and exploring them—is all very useful."

—Edmund White

"Life revolves around sex—reproductive and otherwise. Even those who don't have it react to it and are motivated by it. Almost every relationship bounces off the sexual energy—man to man, woman to woman, woman to man, and so on. I find sex is what everyone is interested in, including myself."

—Morrissey

"I fantasize about being with another man, and I'm not afraid to admit it. You can't help but fantasize about it, if you ask me."

—Dennis Rodman *in his autobiography,* Bad As I Wanna Be

"['The Rectum-Vagina Challenge' sketch]
was an ad parody, the kind where you get people
to compare two different products.
Well, we had the Kids [in the Hall] playing guys
lined up to try fucking these two different holes,
and they had to say which one they liked better.
And, you know, nine out of ten
preferred the rectum!"

—*Kids in the Hall's* **Scott Thompson**

"I can't say by any stretch of the imagination that two men making it would turn me on. If anything, I would probably find it highly amusing."
—**Russ Meyer**

"I am aroused by two men kissing."
—**Madonna**

"When I used to do Vegas shows,
I'd call up Vegas information and say,
'Where can I go to watch two guys
doing it with each other?' And they'd go,
'We don't have any gay clubs here.'
And I'd say, 'Not *gay*—I want
to see two *straight* guys doing it
with each other!'"

—**Roseanne**

"Women in general tend to be more judgmental about what you have between your legs than guys are."

—*Porn star* **Vince Rockland**

"They used to say that if men had sex together, 'What will happen to the baby population?' Well, take a look. There's plenty of come to go around, thank you very much."

—**Gore Vidal**

"A lot of women have had bisexual husbands. But as far as I'm concerned, that means he's gay and trying to pass for straight. And marriages like that don't last. Well, they can... if the wife is frigid!"

—**Joan Collins**

"I don't think straight men who have gay sex for money are gay. I think they're just being paid to do something. There are a lot of gay men who have sex with older women for money, but that doesn't make them straight. It makes them money."

—*Porn star* **Christian Murphy**

"It was like the best of both worlds. It's like you're kissing a woman, but you know it's a man deep down."

—**Dennis Rodman** *in* Rolling Stone, *on kissing a transsexual*

"I don't mean to brag, but I think if I spent some time with a gay boy, he'd never go back to men."

—**Mae West**

15

II Relationships and Promiscuity

"I've never been an anonymous-sex kind of person. I need to know who they are, where they come from, and how many brothers and sisters they have."

—Greg Louganis

"One time I went to a bathhouse
on a Friday afternoon
and met these two guys
and was there
until Monday morning."

—*Porn star* **Mark Steel**

"I have the greatest respect for lust.
I don't believe in simulating bourgeois
marriage. In fact, I don't think
a long-term relationship exists…
it hasn't been tested…until it's been
exposed to—what's a polite word?—
screwing around."

—Christopher Isherwood

"I totally promote promiscuity. I would never condemn it, because I think it's important. Not everyone is promiscuous, but for the people who are, it's an important part of life. To suppress that urge is almost like suppressing your sexual preference, which I think is really dangerous."

—Jimmy Somerville

"I sometimes feel that Americans feel that it's almost a duty to have a good sex life; you know, 'These are my rights, and I'm going to make love to as many men as I can, and I'll feel guilty if I don't.'"

—Simon Callow

"I'm actually very private when it comes to sex. When I'm with someone at the bathhouse, I'm with them. I don't leave the door to the room open, like a lot of guys."

—*Porn star* **Mark Steel**

"I have yet to discover a gymnasium steam room that doesn't smell at least a little of come."

—*Porn star* **Chip Daniels**

"If you want to fuck around, that's fine; I'm not going to be an old auntie and say 'Don't fuck around.' But if you're going to make fucking around your be-all and end-all, don't complain that you haven't found the lover you want."

—**Larry Kramer**

"The problem in this country [the United States] is that people think that gay people fuck and straight people fall in love, which is a complete and utter lie."

—**Boy George**

"Fidelity is a heterosexual
concept based on selfishness.
More relationships and unions
are wrecked by the concept of
fidelity than by any other single
factor. I consider monogamy—
whether it be heterosexual
or homosexual—barbarous,
a most unnatural and
perverted act."

—John Rechy

"We keep thinking that as long as we have a lover and maintain a reasonably monogamous sex life, we are showing the straight world that we are healthy—when all we're really doing is adopting their standards of what health is."

—**Martin Duberman**

25

"Aside from my films, I can count the number of people I've had sex with in my life. I'm very monogamous, and I don't want anyone else playing with my toys."

—*Porn star* **Jeff Stryker**

"The difference between dogs and men is that you know where dogs sleep at night."

—**Greg Louganis** *in the* Philadelphia Inquirer

▥ Parts
Is
Parts

"I'm a homosexual, so of course I like big dicks."

—*Porn star* **Cole Youngblood**

"There are two kinds of gay guys: size queens and liars."

—*Porn star* **Steve Maverick**

"Anyone who finds a penis obscene is forgetting where he came from."

—**Stan Griffith,** *marching in the 1971 Hollywood Gay Pride Parade*

"[Roseanne and I are] watching [a straight porn video], and I say, 'Yep, look at how hung that one is. With a penis that big, he's gotta be gay.'"

—Tom Arnold

"I have a theory that guys who have large penises aren't afraid to show them to other men. I couldn't be gay because other guys would laugh at my penis."

—Howard Stern

"[Italian director Pier Paolo] Pasolini was a man who struck me as being very compartmentalized. He apparently had a very considerable member himself. I've heard that he'd go to these very rough districts and say, 'I bet that my dick's bigger than yours,' and that was the way he got guys to show off to him."

—Terence Stamp

"The dildo people came to me. From what they say, it's the best-selling dildo in the history of dildos. They added nothing in width from the mold from my dick, but they added an inch in length. It insults me that they did that."

—**Jeff Stryker**, *on the Jeff Stryker dildo*

"God forbid a straight person should acknowledge that there are pleasures associated with his anus."

—**Phil Hartman** in Los Angeles *magazine*

"You look at a magazine, and you see this big cock, and you go, 'Wow, it's ten inches long and six inches in diameter, and, wow, it's great!' I think they should make a magazine where they have asshole diameters for stats: 'His asshole's diameter is nine inches' or 'He's got his butt spread six inches apart' or 'He can take fourteen inches.'"

—*Porn star* **Ryan Wagner**

"Your asshole is not a silo for small tactical nuclear weapons."

—*Sex columnist* **Pat Califia** *in*
The Advocate Adviser

"Some of the most interesting things that happen to our bodies are when our bodies change shape. We look down in our underwear and say, 'Gee, look what just changed shape!' That is not such a terrible experience for me."

—**Clive Barker**

"My dad is where it comes from—he has a huge dick. He makes me look like a baby. It's like an old tree trunk hanging down—*wa-woom!* When I was a little kid, it used to scare me: 'Whoa, Dad, put that thing away!' "

—*Porn star* **Jeff Stryker**, *on the genetic origin of his notoriously large penis*

"I was using [a beefcake photo] for fan
mail at Universal. I thought it was a wonderful shot of me. The head of publicity
called me in and raised hell.... He said,
'Look at this—would you want your daugh-
ter to get that in the mail?' I looked at the
picture real hard, and finally he pointed at
the crotch and said, 'Look at that.' Today
people would laugh—there is only a little
indication of my masculinity. Yet in those
days that was verging on porn."

—George Nader

"I see a lot of guys who look real hot. First of all, Brad Pitt is a real attractive man. And a lot of these Calvin Klein underwear models are really hot. I tend to go for the real muscular type—not like a steroid freak, you know what I mean? And a guy with a nice big cock would be fun. As long as he didn't put it up my ass. I don't think I could handle that. I don't even let my wife put her pinky up my ass. I am amazed by butt sex. I think that anybody who can accept a penis in the ass is incredible. It just seems like a torture to go through that. But God bless them if they can do it."

—Howard Stern

"Although there are some gay men who prefer small penises, the boastful phrase 'My new lover has an adorable cock like a tiny pink shrimp!' isn't usually going to make the competition jealous."

—*Sex columnist* **Pat Califia**
in The Advocate Adviser

"Jesus H. Christ! is nothing sacred!"

—**Montgomery Clift**, *reacting to the unexpurgated edition of* Hollywood Babylon *in which he was called "Princess Tiny Meat" because of his small penis*

"I wish I had a bigger cock, but the trouble is, as I got shorter, my cock got shorter. Since I broke my hip, I think I lost a couple of inches. Don't break your hip: I lost an inch and a half off my height and an inch and a half off my cock."

—**Harold Robbins**

IV True
Experiences

"If I wanted a man to know that I was interested, I would put out some kind of vibe. Since I don't, I usually don't ever get any kind of vibe back. But there have been some very... let's say, confident homosexuals who have convinced themselves that they know what's best for me."

—Stephen Baldwin

"When a straight guy meets a gay guy, right away he thinks to himself that the gay guy wants to suck his dick. I say, 'Doll, don't flatter yourself.'"

—Scott Valentine

"I didn't mind Mick [Jagger] sleeping with men at all, and it wasn't as if I was always walking in on him in flagrante with some man."

—Marianne Faithfull

"Oh, God! [Laughs] Can you please just write 'Oliver laughed'? I can't tell you that; I'll be in deep shit. I won't deny it.... That's all I'm going to say on this subject."

—**Oliver Stone,** *responding to the question "Have you ever had a homosexual experience?"*

"Not a real one, not insofar as intercourse."

—**Geraldo Rivera,** *responding to the question "Have you ever had a gay experience?"*

"Gay men don't pursue me, really. I don't send off the right smells."

—**Kenneth Branagh**

"Like a large number of men, I have had homosexual experiences, and I am not ashamed. Homosexuality is so much in fashion, it no longer makes news."

—Marlon Brando

"When I was 10 or 11, I remember
very vividly, I got it on with guys.
But it was just experimentation...I was
a gay bandido."

—**Ted Nugent**

**"Every straight guy should
have another man's tongue in
his mouth at least once."**

—**Madonna**

"Tony [Perkins] couldn't settle down with another guy because he's insecure and craves kinky affairs, not a genuine or lasting relationship. Tony isn't exactly Norman Bates, but he's awfully kinky."

—**Halston,** *quoted in Boze* Hadleigh's Hollywood Babble On

"The only way straight people are going to learn about homosexuality is by being next to it. You can tell them that two men kissing is OK, but when they see it for the first time, it's shocking."

—**Robert LaFosse**

"I went around to the various bars that are in the film [*Making Love*] and hung out there. I was picked up on a number of occasions. I took it about as far as I dared let it go.... I don't think you have to experience a gay love affair in order to play the part. And there's no denying there's a lot of flattery involved there too. If people are hitting on you, no matter what sex, you're getting a nice ego charge."

—Harry Hamlin

"I look at all great bodies. It don't matter. If you see something that's attractive, you have to look at it. I think that's where your mind starts to explore…. I'm not looking at these guys' dicks and saying, "Let me go over there and check it out…get closer and see what it's all about." No, that's not what it's about; it's about the total package."

—Dennis Rodman

"The younger players are really tough to figure. I know two, maybe three guys on this team who have no interest whatsoever in girls. You've had guys like this on teams for a long time, but they're so open about it."

—Joe DiMaggio

"The first day we were on the set shooting [*Philadelphia*], Antonio [Banderas] was in those tight pants and was wearing that cute leather jacket, and I just thought, *I'd flip over this guy. I'd be nuts about him.*"

—Tom Hanks

"[Bob Dylan] once told me he used to hustle on Times Square when he first came to New York, but I don't believe him. I think he was putting me on in order to show how hip he was. But it wasn't beyond his imagination, at any rate, or his sense of humor."

—Allen Ginsberg

"Uh, yeah. We did only two takes, and he wasn't very gentle. And he didn't call me afterward."

—**Matthew Broderick,** *when asked if he had difficulty kissing costar Brian Kerwin during the filming of* Torch Song Trilogy

"I think my first awareness of homosexuality was when the tackle and the guard on the football team broke down a bed in the dormitory. I was 15 then, so I never had the stereotype."

—**Andrew Young**

55

"[Sean Connery, my costar in *The Man Who Would Be King*] and I were in this dumb little town on the edge of the Sahara, and there was nothing to do at night except go to this disco place. But it was all men dancing with men because women weren't allowed out at night. So we're standing at the bar, watching all these guys dancing, when Sean leans over and says to me, 'Do you mind if I dance with your driver? Mine's too ugly.'"

—Michael Caine

"Somebody who works for my management company, he used to look at me and say, 'Ooh, boy!' But I'm very comfortable around him. So we always play around and stuff. He gives me hugs, or he'll grab my butt and stuff like that. But I know him, and he knows me. So it's never really a problem."

—**Mark Wahlberg**

"I've been hit on before. It's impossible not to be when you're in show business. I'm not interested in people of my own sex; that is not my idea of a good time. But if somebody hits on me, I'm not gonna say, 'Get away from me, you fuckin' faggot.' It's not like that. If a person is turned on to me for some reason, I just have to tell him in the nicest way possible, 'There is no hope here; this is not gonna happen here. We can be friends, but that's as far as it goes.' "

—**Frank Zappa**

"Before I fully processed what was happening, [George] Cukor was rubbing my thigh. 'I have a picture in mind,' he said. 'I'm just now doing the casting. I think you'd be perfect for it.' I did not know whether to hit him or to feel sorry for him. Then I thought, *Well, this is not so bad if this is all it is.* Cukor continued with his rubbing, and I pressed him for details.

'Is it a big role?' I asked.

'Oh,' he cooed, 'the biggest.' "

—Anthony Quinn

"I told the story about Eddie Murphy picking me up because [*The Globe*] asked. I have this annoying habit of telling the truth.... It's not as though I'm into outing, but people like him are teaching younger generations homophobia. Discrediting him needs to happen.
He's unhappy, and I hope he gets help."

—*Drag performer* **Karen Dior,**
*who claimed to have had sex
with Eddie Murphy, in* Poz

"I didn't even know a homosexual existed until I was 17 or 18 or something like that. Not until I went to Mexico, and there a blond Norwegian is fair game."

—Starsky and Hutch's **David Soul**

"[Rudolph Valentino] came [to the door of his hotel room]; he had a towel around his middle—a very impressive physique. He was scowling a bit, and his hair was not quite combed—it fell over in little locks—and my heart was going like a...helicopter. And I said, 'Could I have your autograph?'... He took the book and sat down and signed it.... I was about to leave, and he said, 'Is there anything else you want?'... I said, 'Yes, I'd like to have you.'... He reached over and pushed the door shut...and with the other hand he undid his towel. And then he sat down on the edge of the bed. I don't suppose I have to go on, do I?"

—**Sam Steward**

"I've always wanted male friends that I could be real intimate with and talk about important things with and be as affectionate with that person as I would be with a girl. Throughout my life I've always been really close with girls and made friends with girls. And I've always been a really sickly, feminine person anyhow, so I thought I was gay for a while because I didn't find any of the girls in my high school attractive at all. They had really awful haircuts and fucked-up attitudes. So I thought I would try to be gay for a while, but I'm just more sexually attracted to women. But I'm really glad that I found a few gay friends because it totally saved me from becoming a monk or something."

—Kurt Cobain

"When I walked into that room and found
Mick [Jagger] and David [Bowie] together,
I felt absolutely dead certain that they'd been
screwing. It was so obvious, in fact, that I never
even considered the possibility that they hadn't
been screwing. The way they'd been running
around together, and the way David made
a virtual religion of slipping the lance of love
into almost everyone around him, and then the
fact that Mick had a perfectly good bed of his
own just 300 yards away from where he was
passed out naked with David—it all added up
inescapably in my head as well as my gut.
I didn't have to look around
for open jars of K-Y jelly."

—**Angela Bowie**

"I've been conditioned like most people. The idea that there are taboo areas of the body. To kiss someone on the lips is one of those areas. It's a symbolic thing. So all right, I [kissed a male actor in the film *The Grotesque*], and the actor I kissed was the same as me: He'd never done it before with a man. Now we both have, so I suppose we're gay now."

—Sting

"It wasn't that bad. It was like kissing a dog, you know? You know this is unnatural and incorrect, but somehow it doesn't bother you that much."

—**Jerry Seinfeld,** *describing his kiss with Kramer (Michael Richards) on the 100th episode of* Seinfeld

"My father was very cool about my coming out. He said, 'Son, if it makes you feel any better, I've sucked a cock before.' "

—**Alexis Arquette**

"Ever since I had that interview
in which I said I was bisexual,
it seems twice as many people
wave at me in the street."

—**Elton John**

"I tried it once."

—**Richard Burton,** *on experimenting
with homosexuality*

"I've had men come on to me,
but I'm not one of those guys
who gets pissed off and goes,
'Oh, Jesus Christ,
I'm a straight man!'"

—Johnny Depp

"I am homosexual—all of my lovers have been men. Some of them think they are straight, but that's my problem."

—Kenneth Anger

"Bea Lillie is so enchantingly
fey, she can do anything.
I should love to perform
[Lillie's signature song] "There
Are Fairies at the Bottom of
Our Garden," but I don't dare.
It might come out "There
Are Fairies in the Garden
of My Bottom."

—**Noël Coward**, *quoted
in Boze Hadleigh's*
Hollywood Babble On

"Noël [Coward] and I were in Paris once. Adjoining rooms, of course. One night I felt mischievous, so I knocked on Noël's door, and he asked, 'Who is it?' I lowered my voice and said, 'Hotel detective. Have you got a gentleman in your room?' He answered, 'Just a minute, I'll ask him.' "

—Beatrice Lillie, *quoted in Boze Hadleigh's* Hollywood Babble On

"I wouldn't mind having Rob Lowe
shove his tongue down my throat."

—**Holly Woodlawn**

"I didn't get on well with Cary Elwes
[my love interest in *Another Country*].
But love scenes are so much more
magical when you don't get on
with your costar. They're much easier
to do when you don't like the person."

—**Rupert Everett**

"I said to him, 'So was it as good for you as it was for me?' "

—**David Geffen,** *recalling his first meeting with Keanu Reeves after a year of rumors that he and Reeves had married*

"Once or twice when I was younger. Yes [*laughs*]—I mean…no… not exactly…directly… [*laughs again*] But you know how those things are."

—**Bruce Springsteen,** *responding to the question "Has a man ever asked you out or made a pass at you?"*

"I think everybody's curious.… The fact is, up until this point I haven't been drawn to having a gay relationship, and it doesn't seem as though I'm gay. But who knows? I mean, life is a series of surprises."

—Kenneth Branagh

"Not that I know of."

—Willie Nelson, *who recorded the song "Cowboys Are Frequently Secretly Fond of Each Other," responding to the question "Have you ever made love to a man in this lifetime?"*

"I've been in love with women, and I've been in love with men, and whatever people think—well, I think a lot of people don't believe in a thing called bisexuality. I can only judge by the experiences in my own life. I've just always said that I was sexual, and very sexual, because I've had so many experiences with both [sexes]."

—**Dack Rambo**

73

"I do not think Cary Grant was a homosexual or a bisexual. He just got carried away at those orgies."

—*U.S. representative* **Bob Dornan**

"[Costume designer] Miles White…said to me, 'Oh, they have the most wonderful hustlers in this town. They're all straight, they're gorgeous, they'll do anything, and they're $50.' I said, 'Gore [Vidal] said they were $25.' He said, 'That's because he has them before 6 o'clock.' "

—Arthur Laurents

KRAMER: "You once told me that you slept with Tyrone Power."

LAURENTS: "What is this? I didn't sleep with him."

KRAMER: "You did it standing up?"

LAURENTS: "We didn't do it standing up. But we certainly didn't do it asleep. The end. Yes, once we did."

—**Arthur Laurents,** *telling Larry Kramer about having sex with Tyrone Power*

"Yeah, a couple of times. Once by a gay friend who was drunk. It was just, you know, embarrassing for two seconds for both of us, more because he was drunk than because it was a gay approach. When somebody's drunk they have kind of a sloppy behavior. And it was just one of those things where I said, 'No, thank you. I'm just not interested.' "

—**James Woods,** *responding to the question "Have you ever been approached for sex by another man?"*

"If I wouldn't have found Courtney [Love],
I probably would have
carried on with a bisexual lifestyle."

—Kurt Cobain

"I'd rather hang out with straight guys
and not get any sex than hang out
with gay guys and get sex. Sometimes,
every now and then, I score."

—Gus Van Sant

"No, and I'd get embarrassed about it. There have been times when I'll call a friend, and we'll get kind of hot and heavy, and it's late. I don't know. It feels so awkward, and I'll be like, 'Why are you doing this?'... I've tried it, but I'm not very good at it because I never know what to say."

—**Greg Louganis,** *responding to the question "Have you ever called anyone for phone sex?"*

"I fell madly in love with Rock [Hudson] when we were making A Farewell to Arms in Rome in 1957. I had no idea he was gay—I had no idea anybody was gay. He dated me every night, but nothing happened. Lots of kissy-kissy, but that was it, folks. I chalked that up to the fact that he was married at the time and I'm Catholic. So I fell more in love with him because he's principled! Boy, I was really up shit's creek without a paddle!"

—Elaine Stritch

"I was always afraid that at some talk
show they'd take a question
from the audience, and some guy would
stand up and say, 'I slept with you!'"

—Playgirl *Man of the Year* **Dirk Shafer**

"I have nothing to hide. I'm very sexual.
I've been with men, and I've been with
women. I was with a well-known woman
in France, a photographer, Dominique
Isserman, for a year. But I like men too.
Does that answer your question?"

—**Thierry Mugler**

"I thought that [throwing a coming-out party for myself] was the only way to do it. I'd thought of going around and telling friends individually but reasoned that it might be better to tell them all at once, when they'd have each other for support."

—*Monty Python's* **Graham Chapman**

"Father's most recent comment [on *Tales of the City*] was, 'How does an Eagle Scout know these things?' "

—**Armistead Maupin**

"Great sex for me is getting it up."

—**Allen Ginsberg** *at age 64*

"There is nobody in the world that you can't get if you really concentrate on it, if you really want them. You've got to want it to the exclusion of everything else. That's how I got novelist Jack Dunphy. Everybody said I could never get him; he was married to a terrific girl, Joan McCracken. I liked her too, very much. I was just determined. I concentrated on it to the exclusion of everything else. It turned out it was a good thing on all fronts."

—Truman Capote

"[Rex Harrison and I] were commiserating with each other because we were both having marital difficulties. Rex suddenly looked at me and said, 'Ah, my God, Alan, wouldn't it be marvelous if we were both homosexuals?' I said, 'I don't think that would be the solution at all—besides, it's a little late.' "

—Alan Jay Lerner

"I have had sexual relationships with men. I'm proud of that, and I think that it's really important for me to say that."

—**Michael Feinstein**

"I saw some major homosexual activity outside my friend's balcony when I was 5. To this day it's an imprint on my mind."

—**Leonardo DiCaprio**

"I got offers with married couples: guys who wanted me to sleep with their wives, guys who wanted me to fuck them so their wives could just sit there and get off."

—Dennis Rodman

"A good week for me was buggering my sister, fist-fucking the groom at a wedding, and also having it off with the bride."

—Malcolm McDowell, *discussing the year he spent making* Caligula

"I read Larry Kramer's Faggots.
I read some stuff where I was
like, 'Whoa! Hey, you're kiddin'
me!' Kramer's book is pretty
fascinating stuff. At dinner
parties people would ask me
what I was finding out.
'Well, let me tell you...'"

—**Tom Hanks,** *on researching
his role for* Philadelphia

"In New York in the late '40s the *Saturday Review of Literature* had a personals column in it, and frequently you found extraordinary things in there....
I answered one thing which was something like this: 'Should flogging be allowed? Ex-sailor wonders if discipline...' It went on like that and then, 'Write to Bob so-and-so.' So I wrote, and it turned out to be a guy in New York City who was sort of the majordomo of the S/M subculture in the late '40s. There were quite a few people in New York who were available for that sort of contact."

—**Sam Steward**

"A man who managed a horse boarding stable that had several gay customers wrote in. He was sure his customers were having sex with the horses, and he wanted to know if this could expose his staff to AIDS when they groomed the animals or if other men who had sex with the same horses could get AIDS. I told him no to the first question, recommended condoms and a burglar alarm, and scolded him a bit for having such an exotic fantasy about his gay customers. I then got three letters from men who wanted to know where the stable was located."

—*Sex columnist* **Pat Califia**
in The Advocate Adviser

V Speculation and Conversion

"I don't think [John Lennon]
had an affair with Brian Epstein.
I'm not denying it in the sense of
'Oh, dear, no, he didn't!'—but
John wasn't the kind of person
who would have an affair with
Brian and then hide about it."

—Yoko Ono

**"It depends on the intent.
Some people might look at it as
lessening my reputation, others as
heightening my reputation."**

—**John Travolta,** *on whether persistent
rumors that he's gay bother him*

**"Great coach. As a man, well,
I've never slept with him."**

—**Dennis Rodman** *in* Time
on Chicago Bulls' coach Phil Jackson

"After I'm gone, somebody's going to write a book about me that will say I gave secrets to the Nazis and that I had a homosexual affair with Charlie Bronson. Well, I don't really care. The Nazis don't matter much anymore, and Charlie won't answer my phone calls."

—**Burt Reynolds**

"When a homosexual looks at a body-builder, I don't have anything against that.... If I see a girl with big tits, I'm going to stare and stare. And I'm going to think in my mind what I'm going to do with her if I would have her. The same is true of the homosexual—he's looking at the bodybuilder and picturing what he would do with him. You have to face it if you have a good body, and it is somehow a compliment to a bodybuilder."

—Arnold Schwarzenegger

"I act coy when people ask whether or not [cartoon characters] Akbar and Jeff are gay. I say they are either brothers or lovers or possibly both. [Whispering] But they're gay. Actually, I say what would annoy the questioner the most. In most cases that means saying Akbar and Jeff are gay. I mean, it's obvious, right? It's also part of the American tradition: Laurel and Hardy sleep in the same bed, as do the Three Stooges. I rest my case."

—Cartoonist **Matt Groening**

"Well, that's one of the reasons I really respect him."

—**Andy Bell** *of Erasure, relating an apocryphal story about Marc Almond's having to get his stomach pumped after ingesting a pint of semen*

"I asked [Warren Beatty] once, 'Would you ever sleep with a man?' and he said he was sorry that he hadn't but that now, because of AIDS, he felt it was an unsafe thing to start experimenting with."

—**Madonna**

"I'll bet all my money I've ever made—
plus his—that he doesn't have
a mistress, that he doesn't have a gay
lover, that he doesn't have a gay life."

—**Nicole Kidman,** *on*
husband Tom Cruise

"If you are sexually adventurous,
then I don't think heterosexuality
would preclude you from trying
whatever's out there."

—**Hugh Hefner,** *on why he*
had homosexual experiences

"I've never slept with him, so I don't know about that. [*Pauses*] And he doesn't snore."

—**Jack LaLanne** *on Richard Simmons, who said if he got Jack in bed, Jack wouldn't have any muscles left*

"I'm not homosexual or anything, but you're gorgeous! You should get [breast] implants, John, then I'd be with you. We'd finally be together."

—**Howard Stern** *to John Stamos*

"If I believed some of the news-
papers and some of the articles
I read, I'd fear for my safety
right now because I'm sitting
with seven other bishops
who have nothing in mind
but to assault me sexually."

—**Cardinal John O'Connor**

"If you really want to hurt your parents and you don't have nerve enough to be homosexual, the least you can do is go into the arts."

—**Kurt Vonnegut**

"Sure, but actual penetration would pose a slight problem."

—**Johnny Depp,** *responding to the question of whether he would play a gay love scene*

"I really don't care if people think I'm gay. If they think I'm straight or gay, it's great— at least they think I'm going to bed with somebody."

—**Bruce Weber**

"When I was a handsome young boy just starting out, the first rumor people heard was that I was a fairy or a queer or a fag—that was automatic. That was how those columnists could 'equalize' you…. They labeled you with those names, and the hatred behind it was just the same as people who called you 'kike.' I never felt the need to deny anything or defend myself then, and I certainly don't now. I've had close relationships with homosexual men all my adult life."

—Tony Curtis

"You can probably be in love
with a man and not feel any sort
of sexual attraction. However,
if I were a homosexual, I'm sure
I could fall in love
with John Waters in about
a half a second because
he is one of the funniest,
most charming, intelligent people
that I've ever known.
He's really a prime catch."

—Johnny Depp

**"Unfortunately for me,
I did not have an affair
with Mikhail Baryshnikov.
I wish I had, but he's straight."**

—Robert LaFosse

"I've heard the rumors about Tom [Cruise] ever since we broke up, and I have to say, after 4½ years of marriage, I didn't see one sign that he was gay— and I guess I should know! Well, actually, I did hear Nicole Kidman was a transsexual. Now *that* I believe!"

—Mimi Rogers

105

"You can't prove you're not gay.
What can you do,
not blow a guy?"

—Comedian **Norm MacDonald**
to Howard Stern after
MacDonald was gay-bashed
in Greenwich Village

"Me with a guy? Never happen!
[Pauses] Maybe Brad Pitt."

—**Rodney Dangerfield**

Right now I can say
I can probably fuck some guy,
but I don't think I would let
someone fuck me. It would
make me feel like I'm a woman."

—**Dennis Rodman**

VI Pornography and Professionals

"You're flipping through the channels
and you see someone sucking a cock,
and you stop for a second."

—**Richard Gere,** *on the
power of pornography*

"In how many professions can you
go to work every day and
get fucked by some hot guy
with a humongous dick? So I'm
like, 'Great, it hurt. So what?' "

—*Porn star* **Ryan Wagner**

"I had thought I was an exhibitionist, but I found out there's a little bit more to it than just showing off your dick in public. I mean, you have ten people standing around waiting for you to get hard."

—Porn star **Dax Kelly,**
on doing his first film

"A lot of people learn about sex from videos, and that can help them with their relationships or tricking."

—*Porn star* **Coy Dekker**

"Why have a boyfriend? You meet so many cute guys just doing the videos!"

—*Porn star* **Steve Marks** *in* Skinflicks

"A hard-on is my marketability."

—*Porn star* **Dylan**

*"A lot of people put guys like…me
down, but then they go rent
our videos and beat off.
I think those who can, do,
and those who can't, criticize."*

—*Porn star* **Dino Phillips**

"I keep all this shit. I keep it because when I'm an old man and I'm sitting in my rocking chair, a toothless old fuck with my dog, I want to be able to say, 'This was me when I was young—look how big my dick was.'"

—*Porn star* **Dino DiMarco**

"When I jack off at home, I usually come on the floor. Otherwise, you have to clean yourself off."

—*Porn star* **Danny Bliss**

"There's this one corner of my bedroom [carpet] that's probably as hard as a rock from come. I guess it's because I rent that I don't worry about it all that much."

—*Porn star* **Danny Bliss**

"*One thing I like is…guys who are physically demonstrative, who aren't afraid to put a hand on my butt or reach down to my crotch when it's appropriate. Like in a movie theater or an elevator.*"

—*Porn star* **Sean Dickson**

"Most of these guys don't require a lot of makeup, but if they have visible blemishes, such as scars or big zits on their butts or cigarette burns from a kinky trick they took home the night before, we'll have to cover those up."

—Director **Chi Chi LaRue,** from Making It Big, *on preparing models for filming*

"The nice thing about this line of work is you get to live out a lot of your fantasies. A lot of things I do on video, I probably wouldn't do in my personal life."

—*Porn star* **Wes Daniels**

"What do you say to a guy you're balling on the screen when you've never met him before? Polite conversation just doesn't work."

—*Porn star* **Jack Wrangler**

"It's a definite no-no
to go down so far that you
throw up all over your partner."

—*Director* **Chi Chi LaRue,**
from Making It Big, *on
giving head on video*

"My dad did father ten kids.
It's a similar talent."

—*Porn star* **Chip Daniels**

"I pride myself on being able
to please men in bed. It's the one
thing I'm really, really good at.
Even at times when I've met guys
that I wasn't really into and
at the last minute I think to myself,
No, I don't want to do anything,
and it's a pity fuck. You can't imagine
how many guys have gotten lucky
because I'm such a sweet guy."

—*Porn star* **Danny Bliss**

"I don't have to know the guy.
It just has to fit right."
—*Porn star* **Claude Jourdan,**
on his sexual partners

"Now when I have sex privately,
I'm always considering the lighting,
the camera angles, the come shots,
and stuff like that."
—*Porn star* **Derek Cruise**

*"I like a smooth, clean ass.
I don't care if it has a tan line or not.
If my face is buried down there,
I ain't lookin' at the tan line."*

—*Porn star* **Drew Andrews**

**"Jeff [Stryker] won't let anybody
take his dick all the way in his mouth
because he doesn't want anyone
to think that it's possible."**

—*Porn director* **Chi Chi LaRue**

"To begin with, [Jeff Stryker] is short. His dick isn't as big as it looks, and he has a lot of difficulty getting it all the way up. I'm sure I don't have to tell you that he's not too bright. The worst part of making a film with Jeff is the sex. I mean, I had to go home and have sex with someone else to get off!"

—Joey Stefano

"I never realized that it was going to be really bright in the room, you know? It was bright as day. I was just shocked and thought, *I can't have sex like this.* And then they introduced me to the people I was going to be working with, and I got a boner that didn't go down until several days later."

—*Porn star* **Rick Pantera,**
on doing his first film

"Rarely in a movie do I end up having sex on a bed. I'd love to, but they want you in these amazing places. They want you in these outrageous positions."

—*Porn star* **Danny Bliss**

"Just because I took my clothes off and made love in all those movies doesn't mean I don't have any morals. If anything, I'm sort of a prude."

—*Porn star* **Jack Wrangler**

"I'm not really a slut, but acting like one is something I do well."

—*Porn star* **Justin Young**

"I'd never wanted to see any of my work, but I had a couple of roommates who broke into my room and found the video and watched it, so I had to watch it to see what they saw. I remember laughing and feeling very embarrassed."

—*Porn star* **Brett Winters**

"Let's face it, [straight guys] are in it [gay films] for the money. They go in the bathroom with a **Playboy** *to [get hard] to, and what am I going to do, stare at the ceiling fan and try to get a hard-on?"*

—*Porn star* **Eric York**

"This particular one would run out every five minutes, look at a pussy magazine, get his dick hard, run back in, and use my ass as a piece of Swiss cheese—slam it in, get about four good strokes.... If he made body contact with me, he would have to douse himself with rubbing alcohol!"

—*Porn star* **Chad Donovan,**
on a straight costar

" 'Can I buy you a drink?'
It's just so trite. Just once
I want one of the guys
who use that line to say
what they really mean:
'Can I buy myself your dick?' "

—*Porn star* **Justin Young**

"It's a must when you're being blown for your eyes to roll back up into your head occasionally. Your arms and legs should flail as much as is feasible but not so much that you whack your partner or knock over a camera. Also, thrust those hips; it's really hot to look like you're fucking a face. The hands should clutch wildly at whatever's within their grasp: hair, carpet, pets, shrubbery. Every blow job, when it's received on film, should be treated by the recipient as the best one he's ever had."

—*Director* **Chi Chi LaRue,**
from Making It Big, *on*
receiving head on video

"People always want to talk about what it's like to be nude onstage, and it's really no big deal. The hardest thing was the night my grandparents came to see it. I'm onstage, and all I'm thinking about is that these people haven't seen me naked in probably 20 years."

— **Randy Becker** *on his lengthy nude scenes in* Love! Valour! Compassion!

"I do like sex very much.
There's nothing that can top it.
Not money. Not lasagna.
Not even a Lamborghini."

—*Porn star* **Cody Foster**

"A thousand dollars a night—and
more if you want me to move."

—**Joey Stefano,** *quoted in*
Wonder Bread and Ecstasy,
on his hustling rates

"When you're talking come shots, it's tempting to say that more is better, but that's not always so. More is good, no doubt, but for me (and most of the industry), farther is better. It's all about distance. A guy doesn't have to cry me a river if he can send a stream flying across the room."

—*Director* **Chi Chi LaRue,** *from* Making It Big, *on what makes a good come shot*

"In the leather world you almost
plan the sex out. You plan a session,
and you know in advance what
the other person likes and dislikes.
It's almost like going on vacation."

—*Porn star* **Kyle Brandon,**
Mr. Drummer 1997

"**All you have to do is keep those
muscles flexible, then get your dick
semihard and turn it around
and put it up your ass and rock back
and forth. It'll get rock-hard then
and stay up your ass until you come.**"

—*Porn star* **Karl Thomas,**
on fucking himself

"To me, nothing's hotter than seeing an ass getting fisted. I'd love to be able to deal with two hands."

—*Porn star* **Bryan Kidd**

"Pool balls have a good weight—they're heavy, so they don't move a lot, and they felt really good up my butt."

—*Porn star* **Wolff**

133

"When you get locked into being a top or being a bottom, you remove 50% of your sexual experience. We all have dicks and asses, and they were all meant to be used. I feel sorry for the people who don't use them."

—Porn star **Coy Dekker**

"One day my friend asked me if I knew how babies were made, and I said no, so he said he'd show me. Well, we got naked, and he started putting his dick in my ass, and I told him it hurt and that I'd like to get him pregnant."

—Porn star **Gianfranco**

"Who would suspect that if you stick your finger up your asshole when you come that it's gonna feel better?"

—*Porn star* **Vince Rockland**

"I like breaking stereotypes—like the one that all bottoms are skinny half-girls. No matter what you look like, it doesn't mean that you can't enjoy the passive side of sex."

—*Porn star* **Tom Katt**

"It's much less pressure to be bottom. You just spread your legs, and that's it."

—*Porn star* **Claude Jourdan**

"In movies I'm definitely more comfortable being a top. It's easier. You don't have to have that camera shoved up your butt all the time."

—*Porn star* **Wes Daniels**

"First of all, most porn performers are hung better than average. So anyone who wants to bottom in porn must be able to take really big dicks up his ass. Also, since these scenes can take so long to do properly, the bottom must have stamina. A bad bottom is one who stops your filming every five minutes screaming, 'No! Ow! Take it out! Take it out!'"

—*Director* **Chi Chi LaRue,** *from* Making It Big, *on being a good bottom*

137

"**What some of these guys have hanging between their legs keeps me on the top side.**"

—*Porn star* **Devyn Foster**

"You're only as good as your last come shot."

—*Porn star* **Dino DiMarco**

"When you fuck in a movie, it's forever."

—*Porn star* **Coy Dekker**

"I love being gay because I have the choice to suck or get sucked or fuck or get fucked or just jack off or just watch. That's what I love about being gay: having choices."

—*Porn star* **Wolff**

139

VII Pith and Vinegar

"My films are a censorship nightmare all over the world. In Maryland, Pink Flamingos was cut by the censorship board, which we don't have anymore. They cut the blow job and the chicken fuck but left in the eating shit, which, as I've said before, says a lot about community standards in this country."

—John Waters

"Cheetah bit me whenever he could. The apes were all homosexuals, eager to wrap their paws around Johnny Weismuller's thighs. They were jealous of me, and I loathed them."

—**Maureen O'Sullivan** (Tarzan's "Jane"),
quoted in Boze Hadleigh's
Hollywood Babble On

"Don't talk to me about naval traditions. It's nothing but rum, sodomy, and the lash."

—**Sir Winston Churchill**

"Sex is like bridge.
If you don't have
a good partner, you'd better
have a good hand."

—Charles Pierce

"When I told my mother, she said,
'I don't mind, darling, about your being
gay, but I don't want it to hurt
your career.' And I said, 'But, Mother, you
don't understand. It is my career.'"

—Armistead Maupin

"My mother was engaged
to a man, and I had been
sleeping with that man's son.
My mother said, 'Oh, I'm going
to get married to this man,'
and I said, 'Oh, good!
It can be a double wedding!'"

—**Edmund White**

I've always fashioned myself
the all-American queer—
Jimmy Stewart sitting on a big dick."

—*Performance artist-author*
Tim Miller

**"Doesn't 'Keanu' mean
'I like it up the ass'
in Hawaiian?"**

—**Pauly Shore** *from his standup
act, quoted in* Details

**"Men are like diamonds—
they're never too big or
too hard."**

—**Charles Pierce,** *in his
Joan Collins persona*

"I'm really too embarrassed to watch
those male gay movies,
because they're better looking
than I am.
I don't like to see naked people
who are thinner than me."

—**Roseanne**

"Marie Antoinette was not
the only queen in history
who lost her head over a basket."

—**Charles Pierce**

"With AIDS, it's hard for everybody to get laid,
especially in New York, where everyone's
too cool to fuck. But the best thing
about New York is that everyone's cute.
That's why my apartment costs almost
the same as my house in Baltimore:
It's the cute tax."

—**John Waters** *in* Rolling Stone

"It's all about how people insert the penis into the anus and they insert the fist into the anus, etc., etc. That was all very interesting, but it seemed to me that the most interesting question was how the people of Orange County came to insert an anus into the House of Representatives."

—U.S. representative **Barney Frank,**
*referring to a description
made by Rep. William Dannemeyer
of how AIDS is transmitted
—and to Representative Dannemeyer*

"There's nothing wrong
with going to bed with
somebody of your own sex—
they should draw the line at goats."
—**Elton John**

**"Love is as strong as
your condom."**
—**Jeff Stryker**

**"Yes, you can get AIDS
from a mosquito...
if you have unprotected
receptive anal intercourse
with an infected mosquito."**

—Randy Shilts

*"What ever happened to the world-
famous gay imagination? If a group
of people can dress Nancy Reagan
so that she looks moderately attractive,
they certainly can find ways to make
safe sex interesting."*

—Vito Russo

"I knew I'd become jaded when I got bored watching my neighbor across the courtyard fist-fucking his boyfriends."

—Paul Rudnick

"In my deposition the defense attorney asked me how big Rock's dick was when it was erect. And then they wanted to send me to a proctologist to see if I had ever been fucked. And I thought, *What is this, matching the dent with the bumper?*"

—Marc Christian

"I saw *The Sergeant*. You know, the
picture where the officer fell in love
with the young soldier? I got real sore
at that kid. You know, it wouldn't
have hurt him to give in a little
to the old man. And I think it was
silly for the sergeant to kill himself
over the boy without ever having
had him. Who knows? The kid may
have been lousy in the sack."

—Mae West

153

"I don't like being regarded as Michael Hardwick, the infamous cocksucker. There's a lot more to me than just my homosexuality and sodomy arrest, yet sometimes it seems that's all people want to relate to. I'm still being pun-ished for one little sex act seven years ago—and it wasn't even that good!"

—**Michael Hardwick**
of U.S. Supreme Court case
Bowers *v.* Hardwick *fame*

"If a man looks into my eyes, he's looking for intelligence. If he looks at my lips, he's looking for wit and wisdom. But if he looks anywhere else but at my chest—darlin', he's lookin' for another man."

—**Dolly Parton**

"For a woman, to be able to seduce a gay man does much for her vanity."

—**Abigail Van Buren**

155

"I don't get women coming up after
the show wanting to sleep with me.
Gay men want to sleep with me,
but, you know, just for the camp value—
like sleeping with Eve Arden."

—Margaret Cho

"I have the honor of being the only woman

I have ever known to pick up a gay guy

in a gay club. I'm so proud of that!"

—Emma Thompson

"Sex is the ultimate experience in someone's life—when I'm giving it to them!"

—*Porn star* **Jeff Stryker**

"As far as I'm concerned, that is not sex. It's like eating a candy bar through a condom."

—**James Coco,** *on phone sex, quoted in Boze Hadleigh's* Hollywood Gays

"Sleeping with George Michael would be like having sex with a groundhog."

—**Boy George,** *quoted in Boze Hadleigh's* Hollywood Babble On

"Jesus was never married, ran around with 12 guys, and was betrayed by a kiss from another guy."

—**The Rev. Troy Perry,** *founder of the United Fellowship of Metropolitan Community Churches*

"Looks like the guy in my prison-rape fantasy."

—Marilyn Manson *in* Details *on Antonio Sabato Jr.*

"I wouldn't have a problem going to bed with a man or a woman…. In the '60s when people used to ask me, 'What's your sexual persuasion?' I'd say, 'Well, I wouldn't throw Mick Jagger out of bed.' But today I would. Just because he's now so fucking ugly."

—Joe Dallessandro

159

"It was like being on the S.S. *Minnow*—but with just a whole bunch of Gingers."

—*Director* **Jim Steel**, *quoted in* Joey Stefano *biography* Wonder Bread and Ecstasy, *on the ego and attitude that hindered the seaborne filming of* The River

"A lifetime of listening to disco music is a high price to pay for one's sexual preference."

—**Quentin Crisp**